The Illustrated Stories of
Akbar & Birbal

Wonder House

Wonder
House

(An imprint of Prakash Books)

contact@wonderhousebook.com

ISBN : 978-93-89567-83-0

This book belongs to

....

Contents

1

Witty Birbal and the Farmer's Well

*T*wo neighbours, Rahim and Kasim, used to share a garden. In that garden, there was a well that was possessed by Rahim.

Kasim, who was a farmer, wanted to buy the well for irrigation purposes. Therefore, Rahim sold his well to Kasim in return for some money. They both signed an agreement, and Kasim became the owner of the well.

Even after selling the well to Kasim, Rahim continued to fetch water from the well and did not allow Kasim to draw water from it. Rahim said, "I have sold you the well, not the water, so you cannot draw water from the well."

Kasim felt cheated and appealed for justice in the Emperor's court. He described everything to Emperor Akbar and asked for justice.

He demanded that Rahim be taken to task for being dishonest with him. Akbar called his wisest minister, Birbal, and handed over the case to him. Birbal called Rahim, who had sold the well to Kasim.

Birbal asked, "Why don't you let Kasim use the water of the well? Didn't you sell the well to him?"

Rahim replied, "Birbal, I have sold the well to Kasim, not the water. He has no right to the water of the well."

Then Birbal smiled and said to him, "Good, but look, since you have sold the well to this farmer, and you claim that the water is yours, you have no right to keep your water in Kasim's well. Either you pay rent to Kasim to keep your water in his well, or you take that out of his well immediately."

Rahim understood that his trick had failed. Birbal had outwitted him. Kasim got justice, and Birbal was fairly rewarded.

2

Birbal Catches a Thief

One day, a merchant's house was burgled. The merchant was devastated. He suspected one of his servants and tried to find out the truth on his own, but could not succeed. He asked his servants, but a thief never confesses his sin. So, the merchant consulted Birbal and told him about the entire incident.

Birbal went to the wealthy merchant's house and called all of his servants and asked them who had stolen the merchant's things. Everyone denied having done it. Birbal thought for a moment, then gave sticks of equal length to all the servants. "These sticks are magical. They will instantly reveal who the thief is. The stick which is owned by the thief will grow two inches overnight, so make sure to get them back tomorrow morning," Birbal instructed the servants.

The servants went back to their homes. The next day, they again gathered at the same place. Birbal asked them for the sticks. One of the servants' sticks was shorter by two inches. Birbal exclaimed, "This is the thief!" Later, the merchant asked Birbal, "How did you catch him?" Birbal replied, "The thief had already cut his stick short by two inches at night, fearing that it would be longer by two inches in the morning."

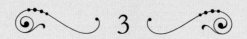

The Red-hot Iron

One day, a rich man blamed a man named Hasan, saying that he had stolen a necklace from his house, and reported the same to Akbar. Akbar asked the man, "What makes you think that Hasan stole your necklace?"

The man replied, "Your Honour, I saw him stealing the necklace."

Hasan said, "No, Your Honour, I am innocent. I do not know anything about the necklace."

The rich man said, "Your Honour, if he is innocent, I can give him a chance to prove his innocence. I will get a hot iron, and if he can hold it with his bare hands, then I will accept that he is innocent."

Hasan replied, "If I am speaking the truth, will the iron not burn my hands?"

The rich man replied, "You are right. God will protect you."

Now Hasan had no other option but to hold the red-hot iron to prove that he was innocent. He asked Akbar to grant him one day to look for the necklace once more. Akbar accepted his request, and he went home. He sought advice from Birbal. When he returned the next day, upon Birbal's advice, he said, "I am ready to hold the red-hot iron, but the rich man should do the same to prove that he is also speaking the truth.

So, let him bring the red-hot iron, holding it in both his hands, then I will hold it in my bare hands."

Now the rich man was speechless. He told Akbar that he would go and look for the necklace in his house again; perhaps his wife had misplaced it somewhere in the house itself.

As a punishment, Emperor Akbar ordered the rich man to give a new necklace to Hasan, and honoured Birbal for his clever idea.

4

Clever Birbal

Once, an oil merchant and a villager began to quarrel over a moneybag. They came to Akbar to resolve their quarrel. The merchant said, "The moneybag belongs to me. This villager came to my shop to buy oil, and in return, he gave me the moneybag." The villager said that he had never visited the oil shop, and that the merchant had stolen the moneybag from him.

The courtiers were surprised to hear this. They were eagerly waiting to see how Akbar would solve this problem.

Akbar called his most trusted advisor, Birbal, to find a solution. Birbal asked an attendant to bring a bowl of water. He placed the moneybag in the bowl. After a few minutes, droplets of oil began to appear on the surface of the water. Birbal concluded that the bag belonged to the merchant and not to the villager. If the villager had not visited the oil shop, then there would not be any oil on the bag.

Everyone praised Birbal, and the villager was punished for lying.

5

Akbar's Dream

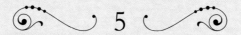

Emperor Akbar and Birbal were in the habit of teasing one another. They never missed a chance to do so. And if they did not get an opportunity, they created one. One day, Akbar was disappointed, as he had not gotten any chance to tease Birbal. So, all of a sudden, he started laughing loudly. His courtiers were surprised.

"Your Highness, may I know what makes you laugh so suddenly?" asked one of the courtiers. So, Akbar started narrating a dream.

Akbar said that he saw Birbal and himself walking towards each other one night in his dream. The night was so dark that they both couldn't see each other, and so they collided and fell.

"Fortunately, I fell into a stream of payasam. And guess what Birbal fell into?" Akbar asked his courtiers with excitement. The courtiers asked in unison, "What, Your Honour?"

"A gutter!" The whole court began to laugh at Birbal. Emperor Akbar felt happy after defeating Birbal for the first time, while Birbal was quiet.

Now it was Birbal's turn. He said, "Your Honour, I saw the same dream last night, but unlike you, I slept on till the end. When you came out of the pool of delicious payasam, and I came out of that stinking gutter, we started looking for water to clean ourselves but did not find it anywhere. Do you know what we did then? We licked each other clean."

Akbar became speechless, and he never tried to pull Birbal down again.

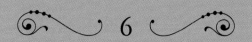

The Three Questions

Emperor Akbar was fond of his wise minister, Birbal. This made one of the courtiers jealous. The courtier had always wanted to be the *diwan* but this wasn't possible as Birbal had filled the position. So, the courtier kept on making plans to pull Birbal down in front of Emperor Akbar.

One day, Akbar praised Birbal in front of that courtier. This made the courtier furious, and he said, "If Birbal answers three of my questions correctly, I will accept that Birbal is really intelligent. Otherwise, you should make me the *diwan* and remove him from the kingdom."

The three questions were:

How many stars are there in the sky?

Where is the centre of the Earth?

How many dumb people are there in

Emperor Akbar's court?

Akbar told Birbal that if he could not answer them, he

would have to resign as the *diwan*.

For the first question, Birbal brought a hairy sheep. He said, "There are as many stars in the sky as there are hair on this sheep's body. My friend can come forward and count them if he wants!"

For the second question, Birbal drew some lines on the floor with chalk and bore an iron rod in them. He said, "This, Your Honour, is the centre of the Earth. The courtier can measure it himself if he has any doubts."

For the third question, Birbal said, "I can't count the number of dumb and intelligent people in Akbar's court because it keeps changing. On days, when people like our dear courtier don't come to the court, the number of dumb people goes down. And when such people attend court, the number goes up!"

The jealous courtier was stumped! Emperor Akbar smiled and told Birbal, "You have proven that you are the most intelligent minister in this kingdom once again, Birbal."

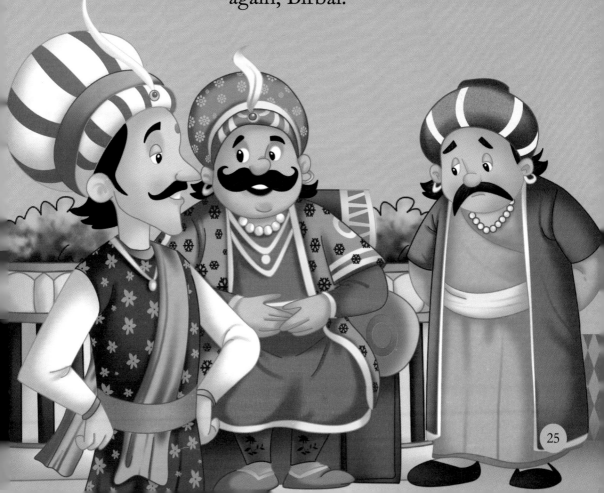

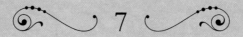

7

The Emperor's Ring

One day, Akbar decided to test the intelligence of his ministers. So, he removed his gold ring and threw it into a dry well. Then he asked his ministers to retrieve the ring without jumping into the well. The ministers were baffled. They thought about it for a while. Unable to find a way to get the gold ring out, they accepted defeat.

Birbal was silently observing this from a distance, but he couldn't resist participating in the challenge. He came forward and said, "Your Majesty, you will get your ring back before dusk." The ministers were amazed at Birbal's reply and were curious to see how Birbal would win the challenge. Birbal went somewhere for a while and returned with some cow dung in his hand.

Birbal threw the fresh cow dung into the well, right on top of Emperor Akbar's ring. Then, he tied a stone to one end of a long rope, and holding the other end, he aimed the stone at the cow dung so that it would get stuck. Having done all this, he patiently waited for the cow dung to dry.

It took a couple of hours to dry, and when he felt sure that the cow dung had dried completely, he pulled up the rope cautiously, making sure it didn't quiver too much. To everyone's surprise, the cow dung came up along with the stone. Stuck at the bottom was the Emperor's ring. Everyone praised Birbal's presence of mind, and this was another feather in his cap.

The Hasty Punishment

During a hunt, Emperor Akbar was once resting near a mango grove when an arrow whizzed past him. He was startled, but not hurt. His soldiers rushed towards him and caught hold of the archer, a young boy, and brought him before Akbar.

Akbar shouted at the archer, "You fool! Why were you trying to kill me?"

The archer replied, trembling with fear, "Your Majesty, I wasn't trying to kill you. I was just trying to hit a mango with the arrow."

Akbar was too angry to listen to any explanations. Without thinking twice, he ordered his soldiers to kill the archer the same way as the archer had tried to kill him. The young archer was petrified and begged for mercy. But no one listened.

The soldiers tied the archer to a mango tree after receiving their king's orders. One soldier steadied his bow and aimed it at the young boy. The boy cried and begged for his life.

"It's unfair!" shouted Birbal, who had been observing the scene quietly.

"You must shoot him the same way he tried shooting our Emperor. Aim at the mango in a way that the arrow misses the mango and whizzes past him."

By now, Akbar had calmed down. After listening to Birbal, he realised his mistake and felt that he was being unfair to the young boy. So, he ordered his soldiers to release him. The young archer bowed before the Emperor and thanked Birbal for saving his life. Birbal had once again helped an innocent man and saved him from Emperor Akbar's hasty punishment.

The Priest's Native Language

Once, Akbar's court was visited by a renowned priest who was fluent in many languages. He challenged everybody in court to guess his real mother tongue, as he could answer questions in any language. Everyone in court thought it would be an easy job and started asking him questions in every language they knew, and to their surprise, he answered them all effortlessly.

Nobody could guess his actual mother tongue and they all pleaded their inability to judge his mother tongue. He then addressed Emperor Akbar, and said, "By tomorrow, your courtiers should tell me what my mother tongue is, and if they fail to do so, I will assume that I am superior to all your courtiers."
After everyone failed, Akbar asked Birbal to solve this problem. Birbal accepted the challenge and assured Akbar that he would solve the puzzle by next morning. Time was granted to Birbal, and the court was dismissed.

That night, Birbal went to the priest's house and entered his bedroom. When he was fast asleep, Birbal tickled his ear with hay a couple of times. The priest's sleep was disturbed, he turned to the other side and slept. Birbal repeatedly tickled his other ear as well. By now, the priest's sleep was totally disrupted and he woke up loudly shouting, "*Yevvurura Adi?* (Who is that?)" and seeing no one, he went back to sleep. Birbal came out of his house unnoticed.

The next morning, the court assembled, and the priest was also invited. He again started speaking in different languages. Finally, Birbal said that Telugu was the priest's mother tongue. The priest was astonished to hear Birbal's answer, and he accepted defeat and left the court. Akbar was curious as to how Birbal had found out the priest's mother tongue.

Birbal revealed, "Your Majesty, a man in distress will always speak his native tongue. The priest did the same thing when he was disturbed in his sleep." He then narrated the events of the previous night. Akbar was amused and praised Birbal for his wisdom.

A Question for a Question

One fine morning, Akbar and Birbal were strolling in their royal garden. Suddenly, Akbar said, "Birbal, can you tell me how many bangles your wife wears in both hands?" Birbal was surprised by this question, and said, "No, Your Highness!"

"Why not? Don't you see her hands every day when you eat with her?" exclaimed Akbar.

"Let's go down the garden, Your Majesty," said Birbal, "and I'll explain."

They walked down a small staircase that led to another garden. Birbal turned towards the Emperor and said, "Your Majesty, you go up and down this staircase every day. Can you tell me how many steps there are in that staircase?"

The Emperor grinned sheepishly and quickly changed the subject as he had gotten his answer.

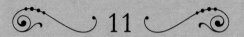

The Last Laugh

As Akbar's most-favoured minister, Birbal could solve many of his problems and answer his questions. One day, they were strolling in the palace garden. It was a beautiful summer morning, and there were plenty of crows in the garden. Akbar was delighted at the sight.

After observing the crows for some time, a question arose in Akbar's mind. He wondered how many crows there must be in his kingdom.

So he asked Birbal this question. Birbal looked at the crows for a moment and then replied, "Your Majesty, there are ninety-five thousand four hundred and sixty-three crows in your kingdom."

Astonished by his prompt response, Akbar decided to test him again, "And what if there are more crows than that?"

Birbal replied confidently, "If there are more crows, then some crows are visiting from the neighbouring kingdoms."

"And what if there are fewer crows?" Akbar asked.

"Then, some crows from our kingdom must have gone on vacation to the neighbouring kingdoms."

Akbar was impressed by Birbal's witty answer.

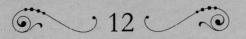

12

A Heavy Burden

A distraught old woman once came to Birbal for help. Birbal, seeing her condition, asked her to sit and offered her water. Later, he asked her, "Amma, how can I help you?"

She narrated her sad story to Birbal. King Akbar had ordered that a palace be built on land that she owned. But she didn't want to leave her residence as it was her ancestral home.

Birbal listened to her patiently and then assured her that he would do his best to help her. The next day, he visited the construction site with Akbar. He saw several gunny bags lying next to a pile of mud. Immediately, he thought of a plan. He began to fill up the gunny bags with mud.

"What are you doing?" asked Akbar.

Birbal replied, "I am filling this bag with mud to earn merit in my next life, Your Majesty." Impressed by his answer, Akbar decided to join Birbal.

Later, Birbal started lifting the sacks and requested Akbar to help him. Akbar was surprised to hear Birbal's request, yet he helped him lift the bags.

"Aah! They are so heavy!" cried Akbar, staggering under the weight of the bag.

"Your Majesty," asked Birbal, "even a single bag of mud is so heavy, can you imagine the total amount of mud there must be on this land?

Won't it weigh heavily on your conscience when you destroy someone's ancestral property? Oh, such a heavy burden it will be!"

Akbar was amazed to hear Birbal's reply, but it made him realize his mistake. He ordered the workers to stop the construction work. Later, they went to the old lady, and her land was returned to her. The old woman applauded Birbal and gave him blessings for his good deed.

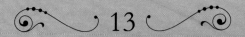

13

The Elephant's Footmark

Once, King Akbar had a tiff with Birbal. It got so bad that he removed Birbal from the post of *diwan* and replaced him with his wife's brother. So, Birbal moved to a nearby village and started living there in disguise.

After some days, the king decided to visit a pilgrimage spot. While returning, he noticed the footmark of an elephant. So he decided to test his brother-in-law, the new *diwan's* intelligence. Akbar ordered him to protect the mark for three days and went back to the palace, leaving his brother-in-law behind.

One day passed, and the new *diwan* sat protecting the mark, without even getting a morsel to eat. He did not get any food on the second day either. By the third day, he had grown quite weak. On the fourth day, he somehow dragged himself to the palace and said to the king, "Your Majesty, I protected the elephant's footmark, as instructed by you."

The king could see that his new *diwan* lacked innovation and was not as quick-witted as Birbal. So, he made a plan to get Birbal back in his palace.

He announced, throughout the kingdom, that all the *zamindars* of the nearby villages must come to him with their wells, else they would have to pay a fine of a thousand coins each.

The *zamindars* were astonished to hear this strange order and wondered how to take an immoveable thing like a well to the king's court.

The king's orders also reached the village where Birbal lived. So Birbal thought of a plan and narrated it to the *zamindars* of his village. The next day, the *zamindars* visited the kingdom to meet the king, along with some other villagers. But they did not enter the court. They stayed outside the city and sent a messenger to the king.

The messenger said to Akbar, "Your Majesty, as per your orders, we are here with our wells. Now, kindly send your wells to welcome them."

As soon as Akbar heard this, he understood that this could only have been Birbal's brainchild. So he quickly sent his people to that village to look for Birbal and bring him back. When Birbal finally returned to the court, the king welcomed him warmly and reinstated him to his previous post of the *diwan*.

Now, the king asked Birbal to protect the elephant's footmark. Birbal promised to get the job done without asking any questions and took his leave.

He went to the village and fixed an iron bar beside the footmark of the elephant and tied a fifty-yard-long rope to it. Then, he sent his messenger to announce in the kingdom that the houses that came within the circumference of the rope would be demolished to protect the footmark. The announcement worried the villagers.

They came to meet Birbal in a hurry and requested him
not to do so. They also offered him a huge amount of
money to not demolish their houses. Birbal said, "If I
do not demolish your houses, how can I protect
the footmark?"
So, the villagers promised to protect the footmark of
the elephant day and night. Birbal collected one lakh
rupees from them and deposited it in the royal treasury.
He told the king that the work was done, and one lakh
rupees had also been deposited in his treasury.

The king was delighted to hear this. He immediately called his brother-in-law and said, "You remained hungry for three days and gained nothing. And Birbal managed to protect the footmark and earn one lakh rupees at the same time, that too within just a day." The brother-in-law accepted that Birbal was indeed the best and worthiest candidate for the position of *diwan*.

14

The Four Fools

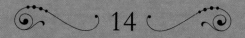

One day, Akbar asked Birbal to find four fools from his kingdom and bring them to him. Birbal was surprised to hear the Emperor's strange wish, and said, "Your Majesty, it's not a tough task. The world is full of foolish people. I will find four in just a few days." Akbar granted Birbal a few days to look for the fools in his kingdom.

The next day, Birbal saw a man carrying a big plate full of sweets, clothes, and precious gift items. Out of curiosity, Birbal asked the man, "Hello, friend. If you don't mind me asking, for whom are you carrying these valuable gifts?"

The man replied, "These are for my wife. Some time back, she left me and married someone else. Now, she is blessed with a baby boy. So I will give these gifts to her."

When Birbal heard the man's story, he felt that he had found his first fool. So, Birbal asked the man to appear in the court whenever invited.

Soon, Birbal saw another man who was sitting clumsily on a buffalo with a bundle of grass over his head. Birbal asked him, "Why do you carry the bundle of grass over your head?"

The man replied, "My buffalo is pregnant. I don't want to put this heavy bundle of grass on her at this time!"

Birbal grinned and said, "Do visit the royal court whenever I invite you."

Birbal called both the men to court the next morning. He presented them to Akbar as the fools in his kingdom. Akbar raised his brows and said, "But these are only two fools. I asked you to bring me four fools. Where are the other two?"

Birbal replied confidently, "I beg your pardon, Your Majesty; the third fool is in front of me. It is you who asked me to bring these fools to you. And the fourth one is me, who took the pains to bring these fools to you."

The Emperor burst out laughing at Birbal's humorous reply.

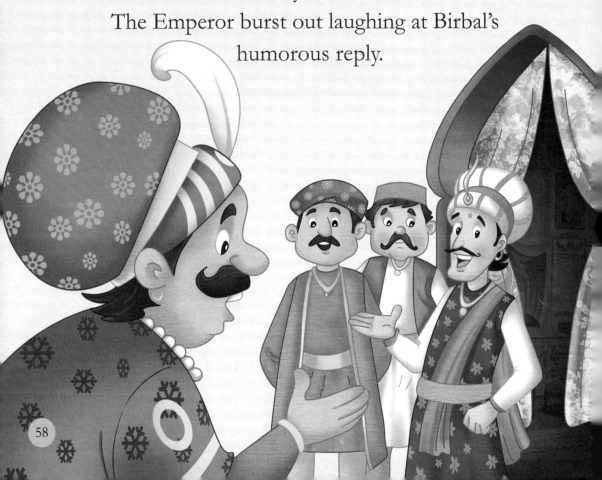

15

Akbar's Lost Ring

One morning, Akbar lost his favourite ring. The courtiers searched for it everywhere, but in vain. Later, when Birbal arrived, the king sadly said, "Oh Birbal, I have lost my ring. It was a gift from my father. Please help me find it."

Birbal calmly replied, "Don't worry, Your Majesty, I will find your ring at once."

Birbal looked at the courtiers suspiciously and then said to the king, "Your Majesty, the ring is here itself. It's with one of the courtiers. The courtier who has a straw in his beard has your ring."

The courtier who had stolen Akbar's ring was shocked and immediately moved his hand over his beard. Birbal noticed this and quickly pointed towards the courtier, saying, "Please search this courtier. I am sure he has our Emperor's ring."

Akbar ordered his soldiers to catch the thief and recover his ring immediately. Akbar was pleasantly surprised at another wonderful example of Birbal's wit and asked him, "Birbal, tell me, how were you able to find the culprit?"

Birbal then told the Emperor, "Your Majesty, I just shot an arrow in the dark. As they rightly say, a guilty person is always scared, so the real culprit revealed himself by moving his hand over his beard."

16

Birbal's Khichdi

King Akbar once asked Birbal, "Tell me, Birbal, will a person do anything for money?"
Birbal replied, "Yes, Your Majesty. A person can do anything for money."
The king ordered him to prove his point. So, the next day, Birbal brought a poor beggar with him to the court. The beggar was so poor that he had no food for his family or himself.

Birbal said to the Emperor, "This beggar is ready to do anything for some money."
It was the peak of the winter season, and the water in a nearby pond was freezing. The Emperor ordered the mendicant to stand in the water all night, and in return, he would be given money. The poor beggar agreed to do so. He stood inside the pond the whole night, shivering badly. The next morning, he came to the royal court to receive his reward.

The Emperor asked the man, "I want to know how you managed to stand in the cold water throughout the night."
The innocent beggar replied, "Your Majesty, I managed it because of the faint glowing light that was coming from your palace, from about a kilometre away. I looked at that light and imagined warmth. It gave me the strength to stay inside the freezing water all night."

Hearing this, Akbar shouted, "You don't deserve the reward. You got warmth from the light, and therefore did not complete the task honestly." The poor beggar went away empty-handed.

Birbal tried to convince the king to be fair to the beggar, but the Emperor refused to listen to him.

From the next day onwards, Birbal stopped coming to the court. He sent a message stating that he would only return to the court when he had cooked his *khichdi*. When Birbal did not appear in the court for five days, the Emperor himself decided to visit Birbal's house. There, he saw that Birbal had lit a fire and kept the pot containing khichdi one metre away from it. Akbar asked, "Why have you kept the pot one metre away? How will the khichdi get cooked like that?

I don't think you are in your senses, Birbal!"
exclaimed Akbar.

Birbal replied, "Your Majesty, if it's possible for a
person to receive warmth from some light that is a
kilometre away from him, then it's also possible for the
khichdi container to get warmth from a fire that is one
metre away."

Akbar realized his mistake. He called the poor beggar
the next day and rewarded him with lots of gold coins.

17

Birbal's Wise Explanation

Emperor Akbar was strolling in his kingdom one morning, when he saw a woman embracing and kissing a child. To the king, the child did not look very attractive, but the woman was calling him the most adorable kid in the world.

Surprised by this, the Emperor called Birbal and said, "Birbal, I don't understand how this woman could shower so much love on such a plain-looking child!" Birbal replied politely, "Your Majesty, the woman must be the child's mother. Every parent finds their child to be the most beautiful child in the world."

The Emperor seemed unconvinced with Birbal's reply. So, Birbal decided to convince him. The next day, in court, Birbal ordered the guard to find and bring to court the most beautiful child the following day.

So, the guard brought a very homely child with unkempt hair and crooked teeth and presented him before the court. "Your Majesty, this is the most beautiful child in the world," said the guard.

The Emperor questioned, "How can you say that he is the most beautiful child in the world?"

"Your Majesty, when I returned home yesterday, I asked my wife to help me find the most beautiful child in the world. And according to both of us, it was our child. So, I brought him to the court," the guard replied courteously.

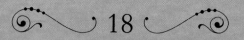

18

Flowers for Akbar

One beautiful day, Emperor Akbar decided to stroll in his royal garden with his ministers. It was springtime, and the garden was full of brightly coloured flowers. There was colour everywhere, bright colours and subtle colours—pinks, reds, yellows, oranges, purples, greens and many more.

The royal poet pointed towards a beautiful flower and said, "Look, Your Majesty, such a beautiful flower it is! I don't think any human can create something as beautiful as this."

Birbal was also there. He said, "I beg your pardon gentleman, but I don't agree with you, sometimes a human can make things even more beautiful than this."

Akbar chipped in and said, "No, Birbal, the royal poet is absolutely right."

The poet continued, "This flower is quite appealing. I don't think there's anything in this world that can truly surpass its beauty!"

After a few days, Birbal brought a skilled craftsman from Agra to Akbar's court. The craftsman presented a charming bouquet of carved marble flowers to the king. The king loved the intricate carvings in the bouquet. He praised the craftsman and gave him one thousand gold coins.

After a few minutes, a young boy came running to the king and presented a beautiful bouquet of flowers to him. Akbar was happy to see the flowers and gave the boy a silver coin.

Birbal was waiting for this very opportunity. He quickly said, with a smile on his face, "Your Majesty, the human-made object was more beautiful than the real thing. Wasn't it?"

Akbar understood what Birbal meant by that. He smiled back at his witty minister and gave the little boy a bag of gold coins as well.

19

Three Words or Fewer

King Akbar once asked his courtiers to tell him the difference between truth and falsehood in only three words or fewer. The courtiers were bewildered by the king's question. When none of them could answer, the king asked Birbal, "I am surprised by your silence, Birbal. You also don't have an answer?"

"Your Majesty, I am silent because I want to give others a chance," said Birbal.

"No one seems to have an answer. So, now you tell me the difference in not more than three words," said Akbar.

"Four fingers," said Birbal. "What do you mean by four fingers?" asked the Emperor. "The distance between one's eyes and ears is the width of four fingers," said Birbal.

The Emperor was confused. He said, "I know that. But how are four fingers the difference between truth and falsehood?"

"What you see with your eyes is always the
truth, Your Majesty. What you hear may sometimes be
false. It's more often likely to be false. That's the distance
one must cover to find the truth. It means that one should
believe their eyes and not their ears. Cover the distance of
these four fingers, and you would be able to unravel the
truth," explained Birbal.

Everyone in court, including Akbar, was astonished by
Birbal's reply.

20

Fear is the Key

One day, King Akbar said to Birbal, "My people love me so much. They are always ready to carry out all my orders willingly."

Birbal smiled and said, "That's true, Your Majesty. But they also fear you."

Akbar frowned at this and disagreed with Birbal. He decided to test Birbal's statement.

The next day, Birbal got it announced in the kingdom that the Emperor would be going hunting, and so people must pour a pot of milk in a tub kept in the courtyard. People thought that the Emperor himself wouldn't be checking the tub. So they poured some water in the tub instead, thinking that the others will pour milk. The next day, when Akbar came back from hunting, he checked the tub and did not find even a single drop of milk in the tub. It was full of water. This disappointed Akbar, and he asked Birbal to guide the way forward.

Birbal replied, "Your Majesty, I will announce again that you are going hunting, but this time, I will mention that you will personally be checking the tub after returning." The Emperor agreed. Once again, the tub was kept, and the announcement was made. The next day, when the king returned from his hunt, he was pleasantly surprised to see the tub full of milk. Birbal said, "And that proves my statement. Your Majesty, it is fear that makes people obey you."

Akbar understood that it was the fear of his kinghood that kept his people disciplined.